The Inside Awakened

Terry Workman

iUniverse, Inc.
New York   Bloomington

iUniverse books may be ordered through booksellers or by contacting:

iUniverse
1663 Liberty Drive
Bloomington, IN 47403
www.iuniverse.com
1-800-Authors (1-800-288-4677)

Because of the dynamic nature of the Internet, any Web addresses or links contained in this book may have changed since publication and may no longer be valid. The views expressed in this work are solely those of the author and do not necessarily reflect the views of the publisher, and the publisher hereby disclaims any responsibility for them.

ISBN: 978-1-4401-9978-3 (sc)
ISBN: 978-1-4401-9976-9 (dj)
ISBN: 978-1-4401-9977-6 (ebook)

Printed in the United States of America

iUniverse rev. date: 01/25/2010

Contents

Foreword

The youth and young adults of today are endlessly searching for something real, pure, and lasting; sad to say, this group searches down the dead-end roads this world has to offer them. The parents of today try every plan and strategy they are aware of that will hopefully intervene during this seeming-to-be never-ending challenge in the home. During this phase, life is packed with issues, causing youth pastors to constantly strive to connect young people to God. This connection will cause a much-needed great awakening. *The Inside Awakened* will address the needs of the adolescent as well as aid the parents in understanding the vital connection between needs, wants, and boundaries that must be drawn.

Tara Workman

Acknowledgments

To my precious wife and daughter, thank you for your faithful love, encouragement, and support. You are both truly God's gift to me.

To my mom and dad, Mickey and Lynn Workman, thank you for your continued support and example that influenced me to reach greater heights.

A heartfelt thanks to my senior pastors, Tommy and Patti Marshall, for constant belief in me leading me in every path of my life.

Thanks to CRAVE ministries, who allow me to serve in this capacity. You mean the world to me.

Thank you, iUniverse Publishing, and a very special thanks to Kathi Wittkamper, who made this project possible.

Thanks to my church family, who are too many to list, for I treasure the relationships we have built since I was a small boy. The newer relationships built are near and dear to my heart.

I want to thank my number one mentor, my Heavenly Father, who continues to give me strength and insight through the Holy Spirit.

Introduction

It came to me in January 2007. Our youth group was on a winter retreat in a remote wooded camp in Northwest Alabama named Bear Creek. To my surprise, the extreme primitive surroundings challenged us profoundly, not only physically, but spiritually as well. I was so proud of our close-knit youth group for beating the odds that stood before them, as the weekend was filled with one physical obstacle after another. Forced to the limit, their courage and unity rose to each challenge. As is most common on all of our youth retreats, our days were exhilarating while our nights became an intimate encounter with God Almighty. This time the Lord led us under the theme of "Destination." The first night was "Destination Forgiveness," in which God challenged all of us to forgive so that we could experience forgiveness. The next evening was "Destination Worship." Wow! Worship was loosed God's power descended in deliverance and just blew our faces off. Our final night was "Destination Not Ashamed." That was our call as a youth group, to carry the gospel of Christ back to our homes and schools. As I remember standing in the back of the room where we met together every evening, God brought vividly to my awareness how He awakens the lives of youth through His Holy Spirit and how there are many things in their lives that are brought to life through His perfect work. I firmly believe that who you are today is a composite of everything that has happened to you in your life as well as the choices that you make. They all have a huge bearing on our divine appointment and destiny.

However, the divine truth is that God is awakening His people to a deeper and truer relationship with Him that goes far deeper than just Sunday morning. Revelation 21:3 says, *"And I heard a loud voice from heaven saying, 'Behold, the tabernacle of God is with men, and He will dwell with them, and they shall be His people. God Himself will be with them and be their God.'"* God's ultimate plan is bringing the fullness of His presence to His people daily, not just on Sunday or Wednesday, but moment by moment with God Almighty. This intimate relationship is what God has intended for us all along. The sad reality is that we have all too often settled for a mere glimpse of the awesomeness of God who is aching to come alive inside us!

It reminds me of a jet fighter pilot who was on a mission during the Gulf War. As he was flying over the enemy territory, he was shot down from a ground-to-air weapon. He immediately ejected from his flaming plane. But as he was descending to the ground below him, he noticed the townspeople and the enemy armies were gathered together, waiting for him to land, waiting to capture him. So in a panic, he maneuvered his parachute in order that he might land on the other side of a hill. As soon as he landed, he cut his parachute chords and ran as quickly as he could into a bush, where he buried his head in the mud. Within minutes, the enemy had come to the spot of the bush and was canvassing the area, trying to find him. Their bayonets were literally coming within inches of his face as they poked through the shrubs and bushes. This went on all through the day. At nighttime, he came up out of the bush and attempted to radio the home base but never got a response. Day after day went by with no contact. When daylight came through, he buried himself in the mud. When nighttime came, he literally sucked the dew off the grass blades for hydration and ate bugs for nourishment. He was hungry, he was tired, and he was thirsty. And as each day passed, his hope for rescue became less and less. He kept trying to radio the home base, but he kept failing. And the more he radioed, the more the batteries drained. It came down to one final signal. He knew it would be his last chance. If this radio signal failed, he knew he would be completely cut off from his rescuers, and he knew the enemy would eventually capture him. So he sent the signal, and just as he did, an ally plane was overhead and received the signal. Within minutes, a rescue helicopter landed directly in front of the bush he was hiding in. When he saw the helicopter door open, he ran out of the bush, sprinted with all his strength, and threw himself across the threshold of the chopper. And as he lay on his back, with his chest heaving and his pulse racing, all he could say was, "Thank you for saving me … Thank you for saving me … Thank you for saving me." When God saves and delivers us, we then become awakened to a new love and relationship with an incredible God!

TERRITORY

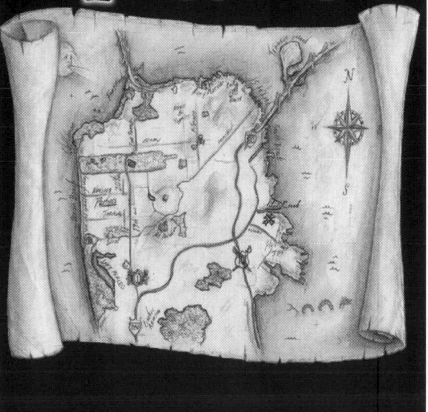

Chapter 1

▼

Territory

It's All about Territory

The most important time in a person's life is their childhood and adolescent years. Here we first discover ourselves as a child, our life limits as a teen, and then what we desire to be as an adult. In this process, we have our society trying to form us to its way of thinking. The media constantly preaches to us with its latest product or fad. What hangs in the balance is the future of each young person. They are either going to be molded for a bright future or led to nothing more than destruction for their lives.

Life is territory. It's all about "my space." That is why our society is hung up on the myspace mentality. You can create an identity and your own little place on the Web that is yours. There is no one to tell you how to act or live your life. It's an exclusive backstage pass to you and your territory. As a teens and twenties' pastor, I will say this: it begins at home. Home is our first and most important territory. It's at home that our day begins and ends. Home is generally our beginning, the birthplace for all that truly shapes our lives. To this Jesus said, *"A house divided against itself shall not stand"* (Matt. 12:25). Here He speaks of the natural place of a home and its physical structure. It is inside this structure that the actual life is developed and nurtured. Jesus acknowledges our need for a healthy home life and the stability it brings to the foundation of all who live there. Good or bad, right or wrong, home first determines all that a young person does or doesn't possess in their personality.

There is the story of John and Charles Wesley. They were very outgoing in their ministries. John was the founder of the early Methodist movement, and Charles was a celebrated composer who was one of England's finest hymn writers and musicians of all time. His songs included such classics as "Christ the Lord Is Risen Today," and "Hark! The Herald Angels Sing." Behind the two awesome ministers was an especially gifted minister at home—their mother. Susannah Wesley both nurtured and challenged her boys. Her father was also a minister, and she was born in England in 1669, the youngest of twenty-five children! Susannah was married at nineteen to Samuel Wesley, another minister. Not to be outdone, she bore nineteen children herself. Her husband was always away at church meetings, plantings, and revivals, so the responsibility of raising their children was hers. She wanted to do big things for God, and she did just that by humbly raising her children to serve God. With so many, Susannah devised a way to spend time with all of them, spending one hour a day praying for all of her nineteen children. In addition, she took each child aside for a full hour each week to instill spiritual character. She trained each child to read the book of Genesis by the time he or she was six years old.

Great things done early in the home can do wonders toward unlocking the mind of a young person in thinking positively and motivating them to pursue a creative future. Sadly, a negative home life can handicap a child. Negative environments cripple and hinder the inner workings of teen's mind, causing him to feel as if they are destined to fail and that nothing positive will ever come from their efforts in life. Home life is the foundation to both the awakening of teens' minds and awareness of God inside them.

God set a precedent in the Garden of Eden when He created the first family. He placed a high value on the family unit by blessing and ordaining the first family union. God knew that the success of the human race would ultimately depend on the strength of the family structure. Adam and Eve would ultimately be responsible for everything that happened in the lives of their children because of the foundation that they would set for them. We see that in their later fall. For in committing the first sin, Adam and Eve broke God's precedent and set into motion negative things in the lives of their children that could not be reversed or taken back. By allowing sin into their home life, they set the stage for rebellion and anger that later influenced their child Cain, which ultimately led to him murdering his own brother Abel. The same goes with us today. As parents, we create a home environment based on our personal examples and actions that work to help mold our children's personality and outlook. God designed it so. Proverbs 22:6 says, *"Train up a child in the way that he should go and when he is old he will not depart from it."* This is a vital truth that works both ways. If we train them up positively, they certainly will not depart from that; but if we rear them negatively, then the same principle applies adversely, and from that they will also unlikely depart. This godly territory of the home is so vital for the foundation to face the issues that a teen will face in their life.

Sadly, this is a very shaky territory. The trends in American families during the past several years reveal that families all across America need healing in this vital realm called home. This past year, 2.4 million couples exchanged these very words in their wedding vows: "I take you to be my lawfully wedded spouse, to have and to hold from this day forward, for better or for worse, for richer or poorer, in sickness and in health; to love and to cherish until we're separated by death. As God is my witness, I give you my promise." These newlyweds are congratulated by well-wishers, with people clapping and blessing their new commitment in marriage. Yet this past year, 1.2 million couples, for different reasons, either separated or divorced. Families today are vastly different than they were just thirty years ago. Back then the traditional family had a working father and a mother who stayed at home caring for their children. This traditional family made up 60 percent of all households in America. Today that so-called traditional family reflects only 7 percent of our households. Now the average American family has one child with both parents working outside the home. Today's parents are having fewer children and having them later in life. More and more households are now blended families with children coming from two or more marriages. Cohabitation before marriage is more common today than ever. One-half of adults under age thirty live with someone before they get married. The U.S. Census Bureau statistics show that couples who cohabitate before marriage are even more likely than others to get divorced later if they marry. Among couples who have been divorced and remarried, 60 percent of their second marriages end in divorce.

The one thing about any territory is that it includes boundaries. Every piece of natural territory has borders—

north, south, east, and west. These borders can also be considered its limitations, or restrictions. The home is no different when it comes to these confines. One of the greatest things I remember about my own home life is that I had borders and boundaries. It is in these perimeters that a young person develops themselves through guidelines and controls. When I was a kid, in my house, the rule for Dr Pepper consumption was one can per day per person. That was the limit. It was not for the lack of drinks for everyone because I can remember cases of soda sitting in the pantry. It was just the fact that the supply was for us to drink and the content was great, but it had a limit and a cutoff point. This made us change our drinking habits to conform to the boundary that had been set before us. We discovered alternatives such as water, Kool-Aid, tea, etc. Imagine the result if we were allowed to drink whatever and whenever. Thus, boundaries force us to deal with things in a way that can help or hurt us.

The next thing that comes to my mind when I think of territory is the covering of authority. It is so important that the territory of the home be completely supported by the authority that produces the boundaries. For example, if Mom said to us boys "Only one drink per day," and then Dad came back and said "Well, you can have two," then the limits would become more like suggestions rather than guidelines. The weight and structure of a rule becomes minimal, and the territory loses its meaning. A child and a teen will push the limits of these lines, testing them to see if they are real or not. The truth is they need limits to teach them that life is full of limits. They are there for a strategic reason that will benefit them. Boundaries are only as good as the authority that backs them up. If children can move their parents, then they can move the boundaries.

Once a young person begins to expand the limits of his/her home territory, he/she begins to look outside it for other restrictions to challenge. This young person will begin to see the world as mere fences they can knock over. Therefore, the territories of the home are probably the single most important thing that we can establish to set life's stage for a young person.

Now that we've talked a good bit about home territory, we must look at other boundaries that a young person experiences in life. There are different stages in these territories. There is a time when a child is allied with the parents. The parents, to the child, seem to know and be able to take care of everything. We all experience this in our lives, where Mom and Dad could do no wrong, Mom and Dad knew everything, and Mom and Dad could fix everything. This territory was at the time of innocence in their lives that they were exploring the limitations of their knowledge because they did not know that anything outside of Mom and Dad existed. This type of territory sets limitations not only on the child but also on the parents, Mom and Dad. What I mean by that is simply this: Mom and Dad began to conform (and the word *conform* means to be fashioned to) to the child's way of thinking, and they develop limitations and restrictions and boundaries on themselves as parents. For example, when you have a small child in the home, it limits the fun activities that can be done outside of the home. You would not take the one-year-old bowling; you would find an activity that would be more suitable to the child at the time. So the stages of a child's life bring a limitation not only to the child but to the parents as well.

After childhood, he/she enters the most unpredictable time of his/her life. So when a child reaches the teenage years, not only is the child dealing with new boundaries and human interactions in their lives, but the parents are dealing with new territorial changes in their lives as well. Parents must broaden their territory and their boundaries too. So the idea of the new territory is not only for the young person, but it is for the parents and the home life of this young person as well. When a child reaches an age of young adulthood, the territory changes, and the boundaries have to change with it. You cannot have a teenage territory with a child's boundaries. They have to go together. When the territory limitations do not change, either the parents or the young person is going to feel alienated from the other. This is the number one cause of a communication breakdown between a teenager and their parents. Either side does not feel that the other understands them anymore, just as we said earlier that there was a time where the child trusted so much in Mom and Dad, but now Mom and Dad seem as if they never have the right answer. This causes a lack of communication in which the parents are frustrated, and in this frustration, they both are not willing to change the limitations of their territory. The good news is that territory limitations can change. But there is a period of time between thirteen and twenty that this territory becomes uncharted for both the young person and the parents who are in charge of them.

So we now know that territory is vitally important to the awakening of a teenage life. Territory gives them foundation—a foundation that they will need when the world of adolescence begins to unfold. Territory with boundaries is even more important. Young people need to know they have a space and area to grow and develop within but that it has limits and they should not cross them. Parents don't hesitate to discipline when the lines of the territory are crossed, just as the Word says, *"Do not withhold correction from a child, for if you discipline him with a rod, he will not die"* (Prov. 23:13). Throughout the rest of this book, I will reflect on this territory subject because we will see the magnitude of its important role in our lives.

How do you view your territory? A shoe manufacturer who decided to open a Congo market sent two salesmen to the undeveloped territory. One salesman cabled back, "Prospect here nil. No one wears shoes." The other salesman reported enthusiastically, "Market potential terrific! Everyone is barefooted."

Love Awakened

CHAPTER 2

▼

LOVE AWAKENED

A young couple was on their way to the justice of the peace to get married when they had a fatal car accident. Waiting for St. Peter outside of heaven's gate, they wondered whether they could possibly be married in heaven. When St. Peter showed up, they asked him if it would be possible.

"I'm not sure, since this is the first time anyone has asked that question. Let me go and find out," St. Peter said.

The couple sat and waited for St. Peter to return with an answer. They waited and waited … for a month. During that time, they began to wonder whether it was a good idea after all, given the eternal aspect of it all. "What if it didn't work?" they pondered. "Would we be stuck together forever?"

Finally, St. Peter returned, looking quite bedraggled. "Yes," he informed them, "you can get married in heaven."

"Great," they replied, "but we've been thinking. What if it doesn't work out? Could we also get divorced in heaven?"

Suddenly St. Peter threw his clipboard down and glared at them.

"What's wrong?" asked the frightened couple.

"Give me a break!" St. Peter yelled. "It just took me a month to find a preacher that would take a chance on the first marriage in heaven! Have you any idea how long it would take me to find a lawyer up here?"

Just as I mentioned before, we will be discussing the different territories of a young person's life. One of the most delicate territories of a young person's life is the territory of love. It's this territory the changes so rapidly in their lives. For example, a child experiences love with Mom and Dad when they're young, a level of nurturing and caring that is appropriate for that time. And as the child reaches the age of accountability, that love comes with responsibility, and then the discipline process begins. Then as this young person reaches the age of adolescence, they begin to search for a love with a greater level of affection. This territory changes, and out of it comes an awakening to a love that they have never known before but desire to take hold of for themselves. This is where most teenagers fall into the trap of lust. The devil wants to distract and destroy them to his fullest ability (John

10:10). He begins to play the lust card and dresses it up to be so close to love that it becomes appetizing to a person that is going through a territory change in their life. He uses society, the media, peer pressure, and, as always, the home to distract from the true meaning of love. Once a teenager establishes his/her territorial boundaries, that then sets a precedent for the rest of his/her life. We sometimes take for granted that if we love them and they know the love that we give them as children, then they will automatically know and find true love. This could not be any farther from the truth. The truth is that even if parents love and do everything for their child while he/she young, it doesn't excuse them from the territorial change that will take place in their lives. So we have to be conscious of this and continue teaching and developing our young people to the only love they can trust, and that is *God!*

There is such a powerful meaning inside the four letters that make up the word *love*. It almost seems that everyone, at some point or another, has been on a quest to discover its true meaning. From the time that you and I were born, we have sought true love and affection. The word *love* is mentioned 280 times in the Bible. Its words command us to fulfill the mandate of its great calling. We were created to love. Our young and innocent selves first longed for the love and affection of Mom and Dad. Whether they were present or not, we still pursue the love and affection of our parents.

A prime example is this: we were created to love God and have intimacy with Him. Have you ever wondered why an addict becomes addicted to a feeling or a way of life that is destroying them? It's simple—they are fulfilling a desire to love something and be accepted by people whom they feel care for them. This endeavor to find true love has carried many people in different directions of life. In short, life is the ship, and our love and passion is the current with which we will flow. The most frightening area for a person is when they come to a place in their life where they're disarming the love that they grew up knowing for Mom and Dad into a new design of what love will mean to them for the rest of their lives. Love has many different designs, many different forms, and many different shapes, so a young person has to adapt smoothly to the transitions of these phases. I do love my dog, my wife, and my daughter; however, I love each of them differently because of the different designs of love. The sad truth of the matter is that the devil can take these different shapes and forms to deceive our young people today. His goal is to deceive and to copycat what God has predestined for our young people to have in His perfect love.

1 Corinthians 13:1–8

Though I speak with the tongues of men and of angels, but have not love, I have become sounding brass or a clanging cymbal.

And though I have the gift of prophecy, and understand all mysteries and all knowledge, and though I have all faith, so that I could remove mountains, but have not love, I am nothing.

And though I bestow all my goods to feed the poor, and though I give my body to be burned, but have not love, it profits me nothing.

Love suffers long and is kind; love does not envy; love does not parade itself, is not puffed up;

Love does not behave rudely, does not seek its own, is not provoked, and thinks no evil; Love does not rejoice in iniquity, but rejoices in the truth;

Love bears all things, believes all things, hopes all things, and endures all things.

Love never fails.

In 1 Corinthians 13, we read a very detailed description of what the Bible says that love is. For a young person, it's not always that cut-and-dried. They're bombarded with society's viewpoint of what love should be and how love should feel a high risk of emotions that are involved in the world's view of love. Our society is full of a "love equals sex" mentality that forces our teens to believe that love is a physical happening rather than a God-planned event. They are thought this worldview through the media, TV shows, movies, magazines, and commercials. Almost 90 percent of the commercials on TV are showing a picture of a sexy person advertising a product that has nothing to do with sex. We have become a sex-driven society. Sadly, right in the middle of this is the life of a young person who is experiencing this awakening in their life for the first time to this level.

We all grew up with that unconditional love for Mom and Dad. Then teen life hits, and we discover that there is more to love than what we know at that point. *Storge*—a Greek word referring to love found among family members, the kind of love found between a parent and child. This love is a strong love, a "die for you" kind of love, which is the stage that most of us remember and know. However, there is a time in which a young person needs to know the other kinds of love that they are being awakened to in their lives.

Allow me to give you just one thought that will sum up a young person's view on love. If I told you "I love you" every day and I followed it with a physical strike to your body, then you would associate love with abuse. The next time someone says to you "I love you," then you would automatically be expecting the abuse to follow. It is the same principle with us today that we associate events, circumstances, and people with love that gives us our own definition of love. *Love* is the only word that if you ask ten people the definition to you will probably get ten different answers. I see this in youth ministry so often, not just with youth but with their parents as well. I tell a young person "I love you, and so does God," and then I get a look of confusion because someone or something has given them a different perspective on love than what God has intended for them. Jesus understood the power of love; in John 13:35, He said, *"By this shall all men know that ye are my disciples, if ye have love one to another."* Jesus knew that true love was a direct reflection of Himself and the Father, and it was up to the church to portray that love in its purest form. In a nutshell, they can't understand when I say "I love you" that I mean "with God's love" because to them, love could mean abuse, abandonment, neglect, or even addiction. By the time a person reaches the age of adolescence, they have such a mixture of what love is that they become a prime target for Satan to begin to deceive and pull them away.

William Gladstone, in announcing the death of Princess Alice to the House of Commons, told a touching story. The little daughter of the princess was seriously ill with diphtheria. The doctors told the princess not to kiss her little daughter and endanger her life by breathing the child's breath. Once, when the child was struggling to breathe, the mother, forgetting herself entirely, took the little one into her arms to keep her from choking to death. Rasping and struggling for her life, the child said, "Momma, kiss me!" Without thinking of herself, the mother tenderly kissed her daughter. She got the diphtheria, and some days thereafter, she went to be forever with the Lord. Real love forgets self. Real love knows no danger. Real love doesn't count the cost. The Bible says in Song of Solomon 8:7, *"Many waters cannot quench love, neither can the floods drown it."*

John 4:8 says that God is love. So God being the ultimate love, and because we are trying to understand that love, then we must understand God first and the depth of the love He has. Now if you replace the word *love* in 1 Corinthians 13 with the word *God*, then we will get an awesome description of what love really means.

> Though I speak with the tongues of men and of angels, but have not GOD, I have become sounding brass or a clanging cymbal.
> And though I have *the gift of* prophecy, and understand all mysteries and all knowledge, and though I have all faith, so that I could remove mountains, but have not GOD, I am nothing.
> And though I bestow all my goods to feed *the poor,* and though I give my body to be burned, but have not GOD, it profits me nothing.

GOD suffers long *and* is kind; GOD does not envy; GOD does not parade Himself, He is not puffed up;
GOD does not behave rudely, He does not seek its own, He is not provoked, thinks no evil;
GOD does not rejoice in iniquity, but rejoices in the truth;
GOD bears all things, believes all things, hopes all things, and endures all things.
GOD never fails.

John 15:13: *Greater love has no one than this, than to lay down one's life for his friends.*

So love awakened for the first time in someone's life can be a new, life-changing experience that can leave questions and new adventures.

There was a pastor, who after the usual Sunday evening hymns stood up, walked over to the pulpit, and, before he gave his sermon for the evening, briefly introduced a guest minister who was in service that evening. In the introduction, the pastor told the congregation that the guest minister was one of his dearest childhood friends and that he wanted him to have a few moments to greet the church and share whatever he felt would be appropriate for the service. With that, an elderly man stepped up to the pulpit and began to speak.

"A father, his son, and a friend of his were sailing off of the Pacific Coast," he began, "when a fast-approaching storm blocked any attempt to get back to shore. The waves were so high that even though the father was an experienced sailor, he could not keep the boat upright, and the three were swept into the ocean as the boat capsized." The old man hesitated for a moment, making eye contact with two teenagers who were, for the first time since the service began, looking somewhat interested in his story.

The aged minister continued with his story. "Grabbing a rescue line, the father had to make the most excruciating decision of his life: to which boy he would throw the other end of the lifeline. He only had seconds to make the decision. The father knew that his son was a Christian, and he also knew that his son's friend was not. The agony of his decision could not be matched by the torrent of the waves. As the father yelled out 'I love you, son!' he threw out the lifeline to his son's friend. By the time the father had pulled the friend back to the capsized boat, his son had disappeared beneath the raging swells into the black of the night. His body was never recovered."

By this time, the two teenagers were sitting up straight in the pew, anxiously waiting for the next words to come out of the old minister's mouth. "The father," he continued, "knew his son would step into eternity with Jesus, and he could not bear the thought of his son's friend stepping into eternity without Jesus. Therefore, he sacrificed his son to save his son's friend." With that the old man turned and sat back down in his chair as silence filled the room.

The pastor again walked slowly to the pulpit and delivered a brief sermon. Within minutes after the service ended, the two teenagers were at the old man's side. "That was a nice story," the boys stated politely. "But I don't think it was realistic for a father to give up his son's life in hopes that the other boy would become a Christian," one of the teenagers said.

"Well, you've got a point there," the old man replied, glancing down at the worn Bible. A big smile broadened his narrow face. He once again looked up at the boys and said, "It sure isn't realistic, is it? But I'm standing today to tell you that the story gives me a glimpse of what it must have been like for God to give up His only son for me. You see, I was the father, and your pastor was my son's friend."

An awakening of true love only comes from a true God!

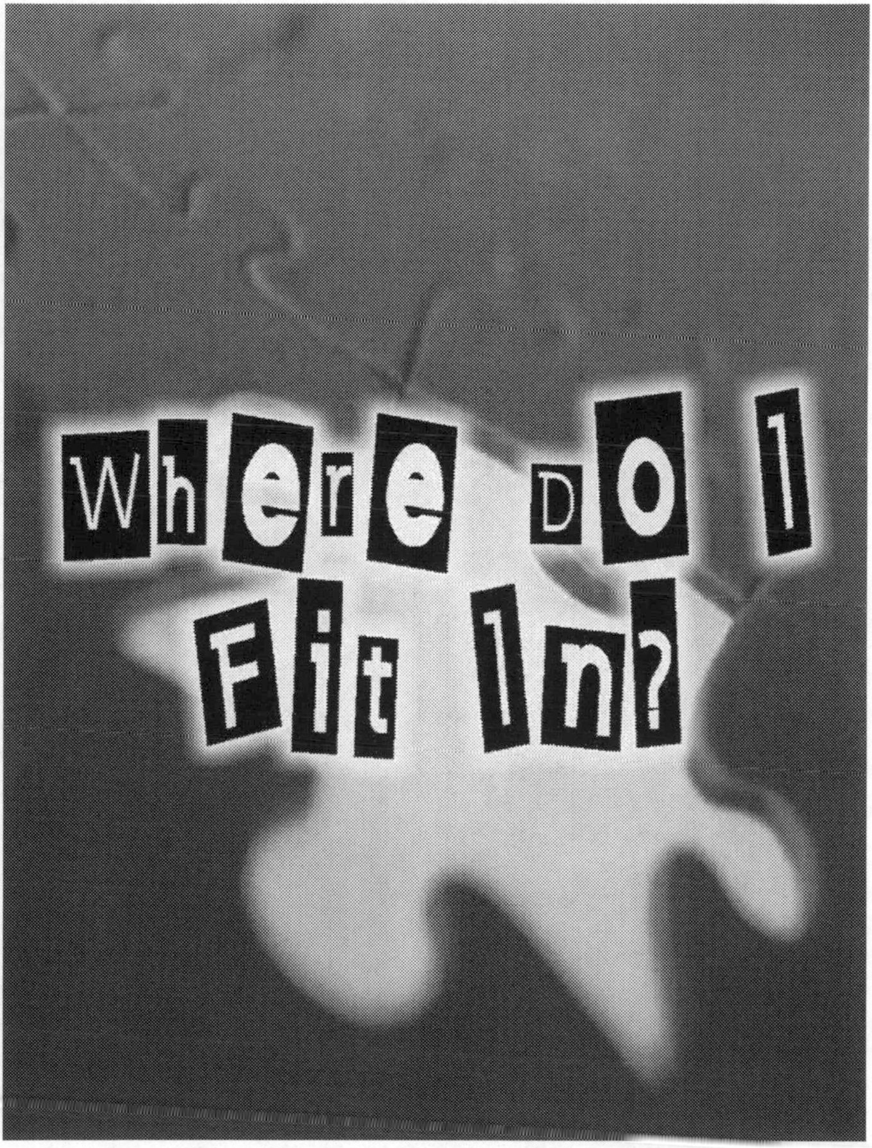
Where Do I
Fit In?

▼

CHAPTER 3

WHERE DO I FIT IN?

One Sunday morning, a mother went in to wake her son and tell him it was time to get ready for church, to which he replied, "I'm not going."

"Why not?" she asked.

"I'll give you two good reasons," he said. "One, they don't like me; and two, I don't like them."

His mother replied, "I'll give *you* two good reasons why you *should* go to church. One, you're fifty-four years old; and two, you're the pastor!"

Isaiah 43:7 says, *"Everyone who is called by My name, whom I have created for My glory; I have formed him, yes, I have made him."* Have you ever met someone who just doesn't fit in? Sure you have, we all have. I can't say this enough: *You have a purpose in this life.* Every one of us has a specific and useful assignment that God has purposely planned and custom made for our lives. It's our destiny and our "home." In 2 Timothy 2:21, it says, *"Therefore if anyone cleanses himself from the latter, he will be a vessel for honor sanctified and useful for the Master, prepared for every good work."*

For a person to think they don't fit in or don't have a purpose means they think God made a mistake and God never makes mistakes. God strategically placed you here for an assignment that only you can fulfill. Everything has been created with a purpose. Example: ears to hear, eyes to see, legs to walk. I could go on and on because everything has a purpose. Everyone has an assignment, and sadly, the devil is more committed to seeing our purpose destroyed than we are seeing it completed. Inside our territory, we must find our purpose. This can be discouraging and difficult because our current environment isn't always our destiny. But since we are products of our environment, then we tend to adapt to where we are. For example, the great white shark has a potential to be more than 20 feet long and weigh up to 4,960 pounds. However, if you were to put a baby great white in a small fish tank, then it would only grow to the size of the tank and never reach its potential. We are a product of our environment, but our potential is so much greater in God.

Everything is most vulnerable at its earliest stage. Children, ministries, businesses, marriages, and friendships all begin and have their most trying and testing times early in their cycle. I see this so many times with new Christians who get saved and God does so much for them, and then within the first three months of their walk with the Lord, they end up giving up. People who experience this quick discouragement are often asking the question, "Where do I fit in?" Eighty percent of Christians come to Jesus in their teens; it's the most record-setting time for your life. Only 20 percent of Christians today make the conversion after their adolescent years.

Former senator Dwight W. Morrow searched in vain to find his railroad ticket as he was on a train leaving New York City. "I must find that ticket," he muttered. The conductor who stood waiting beside him said, "Don't worry about it, Mr. Morrow. We know you had a ticket. Just mail it to the railroad when you find it."

"That's not what's troubling me," replied Morrow. "I need to find it to know where I'm going."

How many of us have been in that place where we know we have a purpose but we feel that we just don't know what it is?

One of the devil's main devices is to make a person feel displaced or abandoned—it's only when a person feels out of place that they begin looking for a new home. We begin looking for a new destiny instead of what God has for us, and that is when Satan is lying in wait. You take a young person, or even an adult, who for the most part of their life, due to territorial issue in the home, has been isolated from true love and acceptance, and they are then sucked into a lifestyle of hopeless encounters with a failed substitute of their place in life. This is the gang mentality; this is why so many people join gangs, clubs, and ritualistic organizations. This is where they can find acceptance just as they are without any explanation of their lifestyle or actions. It is the thought of "I can be who I want to be, and that is okay. I just want to be accepted at any cost."

Our society today is plagued with the "emo" movement. This is the group that thinks its okay to cut themselves and take out their frustrations in life on the physical body in hopes to get revenge for a lack of love and nurturing from their past. The hard core of it is that our kids today are taking the hurts out on themselves as if they are to blame for the shortcomings of a broken home in which their territorial boundaries were unstable. Guys and girls alike are cutting and torturing their bodies just to satisfy the grieving of their soul. It's a demonic stronghold that Satan has and he is determined to kill our young people; and quite frankly, he doesn't care! I see this all too often as a youth pastor. My biggest adversary besides Satan himself is the home. I preach love, compassion, and righteousness; and the home life teaches that it's okay to drink and curse and have premarital sex, and the parents leave it up to the church to "straighten" their kids out. We are living in a day and time where God wants our homes to be a confirmation of what the church is preaching and teaching, not a contradiction. Parents, it is time to rise to the occasion and begin helping your local church in the battle for the soul of your child. Don't misunderstand me, there are some great parents out there, and not all are doing what I am talking about, but it would shock you to know the statistics of the ones who are. This causes a young person to say, "Where do I fit in?" Home says this, and the church speaks of something different. They are torn and without a foundation. So they begin to find an acceptance elsewhere, with no regard to the consequences of their decisions.

I would like to take your attention to the Word of God for a moment and look at some scripture about a young man who felt abandoned and out of place. The story begins first in 2 Samuel 4:4.

2 Samuel 4:4

Jonathan, Saul's son, had a son who was lame in his feet. He was five years old when the news about Saul and Jonathan came from Jezreel, and his nurse took him up and fled. And it happened, as she made haste to flee, that he fell and became lame. His name was Mephibosheth.

Mephibosheth is the son of Jonathan and the grandson of King Saul. Saul and Jonathan were off in battle when tragedy strikes and both of them are killed in the line of duty. In the haste of this gruesome news, Mephibosheth's babysitter grabs everything she can in preparation to flee for safety. She drops him, and instantly he becomes lame in both feet. So all in one day, he goes from prince to poverty. He loses his dad, granddad, his inheritance, and his ability to walk.

Wow! Have you ever felt that way? Mephibosheth found himself in the middle of a circumstance that was *not* his fault. This is so familiar with people today; we all have found ourselves in a place where the circumstance is completely out of our control. Mom and Dad are divorcing, or Dad lost his job; maybe a tragic accident has taken a parent out of one's life, causing them to be in a situation that is completely not their fault. A great number of people in our society today find themselves in a place where they feel that they don't fit in because of something that has happened to them that is out of their control. So they begin to dwell on the result of their circumstance and accept the fact that they are spiritually and emotionally crippled. Here is a young man who had a purpose and a destiny. Like many of us when we were formed in the womb, he had a heritage of royalty that would be his ultimate covering. Then without warning, he is struck with an event in his life that would cause him to be displaced and pushed aside. However, God has a plan. I believe that it was the nature of his circumstance that caused him to see the value of his inheritance. So many times God is trying to get our attention by allowing a circumstance to temporarily cripple us so we will realize that we do have a place in His perfect plan. It is only when we fail to see God that we fail to find our place in life. Mephibosheth had to realize that his place in life was up to the King.

2 Samuel 9:1–13

Now David said, "Is there still anyone who is left of the house of Saul, that I may show him kindness for Jonathan's sake?"

And *there was* a servant of the house of Saul whose name *was* Ziba. So when they had called him to David, the king said to him, "*Are* you Ziba?"

He said, "At your service!"

Then the king said, "*Is* there not still someone of the house of Saul, to whom I may show the kindness of God?"

And Ziba said to the king, "There is still a son of Jonathan *who is* lame in *his* feet."

So the king said to him, "Where *is* he?"

And Ziba said to the king, "Indeed he *is* in the house of Machir the son of Ammiel, in Lo Debar."

Then King David sent and brought him out of the house of Machir the son of Ammiel, from Lo Debar.

Now when Mephibosheth the son of Jonathan, the son of Saul, had come to David, he fell on his face and prostrated himself. Then David said, "Mephibosheth?"

And he answered, "Here is your servant!"

So David said to him, "Do not fear, for I will surely show you kindness for Jonathan your father's sake, and will restore to you all the land of Saul your grandfather; and you shall eat bread at my table continually."

Then he bowed himself, and said, "What *is* your servant, that you should look upon such a dead dog as I?"

And the king called to Ziba, Saul's servant, and said to him, "I have given to your master's son all that belonged to Saul and to his entire house.

You therefore, and your sons and your servants, shall work the land for him, and you shall bring in *the harvest,* that your master's son may have food to eat. But Mephibosheth your master's son shall eat bread at my table always." Now Ziba had fifteen sons and twenty servants.

Then Ziba said to the king, "According to all that my lord the king has commanded his servant, so will your servant do."

"As for Mephibosheth," *said the king,* "he shall eat at my table like one of the king's sons."

Mephibosheth had a young son whose name *was* Micha. And all who dwelt in the house of Ziba *were* servants of Mephibosheth.

So Mephibosheth dwelt in Jerusalem, for he ate continually at the king's table. And he was lame in both his feet.

King David didn't have to restore him or reconcile any properties back to him. His decision to do so was solely on the covenant relationship that he had with his dad and his granddad. *Wow!* This so true today. God is bound to his covenant that he establishes in us to perform and carry out His plan for our lives. It was not by any merit or duty performed by Mephibosheth—it was purely a bond of love. God wants us to have what He has committed to us to have, but we must first realize that we may have had some things happen that are out of our control, and yes that does hurt. However, God is in the restoration business. It's a part of His plan to awaken His people to His glory. For us to realize that our position in life and our assignment is completely in His control no matter where circumstances place us in life or what we lose or gain. God is not moved by self-pity or a poor-ole-me attitude. If you noticed that even after the restoration of Mephibosheth he was still lame, that tells us that we might still remember the hurts and pains of our lives that we could not control, but God wants us to have a greater view of Him than our problems of the past.

We often view our destiny as a mystical place of enchantment that is always out of reach. I believe that destiny is a now event. My personal equation for destiny is 5 percent past, 5 percent future, and 90 percent present. I think that it is in the *now* moments of life in which you make destiny come to you rather than you chasing after a fantasy. God has a very specific purpose, calling, and mantle for you. Maybe you're finding yourself right now in a place, spiritually or physically, where you don't quite belong. Where you are struggling and gasping for breath, like a fish floundering around on the shore. Take that fish and put it in the water, and its genius emerges! It does what it was called to do—it swims away gracefully and purposefully. You weren't made to flounder around. You have a specific purpose in the church and in God's Kingdom. You might think that if you don't step into that calling, someone else will do it. You might think that the church has others much more gifted than you. "Certainly, my pathetic talents won't make any difference." Oh, beloved, you're wrong. A Rolls-Royce is a beautiful car, a very expensive and luxurious car. A Rolls-Royce with three wheels is limited, so too the church, and the Kingdom, without you. Each of us has a very specific and unique calling which is important to the whole. I used to think that if I didn't participate, so what? God will anoint and commission someone else. I was wrong. If I don't fulfill my calling, if you don't fulfill yours, the church will go without. I cannot be all that I was called to be unless you become all that you are called to be. Besides, you and I don't have the right to hold anything back from Him who gave everything for us, do we? Ezekiel 16:60 says, *"Nevertheless, I will remember My covenant with you in the days of your youth, and I will establish an everlasting covenant with you."*

Desperate To Be Awakened

Chapter 4

▼

Desperate to be Awakened

It is amazing how desperation will drive us to or away from something in our lives. Desperation will cause us to push the limits of our territory. It will cause us to look for love in places that it does not exist, or maybe even make us feel out of place. We all have been in a place where desperation was our biggest driving force. What would *you* be willing to do for a large sum of money? Maybe ... fudge a little on your taxes? Tell your insurance company a story that wasn't the whole truth? Let's forget about cash. What would you be willing to do to find a cure for cancer? How about world peace, or ending hunger? What would you do to save your best friend's life?

When disaster seems to haunt us and we are faced with circumstances that are devastating, over and over again, areas of our lives seem to continuously erupt in turmoil. These are desperate times, calling for desperate measures. What do we do, then? When we repeatedly face disaster in an area of our lives, when we seem to be using all of our resources to recover from a tragedy, only to have another horrible attack, in the same area, come upon us. What do we do when life beats us down, when after rallying to face our enemy once and beat it back, it rises up to attack us again? Then we face it down again, only to have it come up another way, from another direction. Then we rally our defenses, only to have it come back, the cycle going on again and again. Each time we go through it, we find that our resources, our strength, and our energy to face the attacks grow smaller and smaller. Until finally, there is nothing left, what do we do, then?

Have you ever seen an episode of COPS? Each episode is packed full of desperate people doing absurd crimes that anyone with a clue to life would see a sure capture and punishment. The only reason they think this way is because they are desperate, so desperate that they don't have any thought for the future or their well-being. Our society is full of desperate people, desperately wanting to be loved, accepted, respected, and valued for who they are, not for what people perceive them to be. Our mentality today is "The more desperate you are, then the more valuable you are to everyone else." This is most dominant in the work field of America. If you are willing to do the "dirty work" of a boss or a company, then you are possibly a good asset to the business because your desperation for your job causes you to have no moral or ethical boundaries. Desperation is a very powerful and persuasive place in which we all have been before.

If we are not careful, we will find ourselves in a state of mind where we are desperate to fill the void in our lives that only God can fill. Desperate people take desperate measures. In our society, you find people getting into more and more deception because of the lack of awakening to God in their lives. Myspace, the emo movement, and the entire media are nothing more than desperate people leading on other desperate people by or through their emotions. I believe that in order to get the fullness of God in our lives, we have to be desperate for Him. We must be desperate to see the entire plan that He has for our lives. God is not moved by a need in our lives, but He is moved by the desperation in our hearts to trust Him and surrender to His will for us.

Mark 5:25–34

Now a certain woman had a flow of blood for twelve years,

and had suffered many things from many physicians. She had spent all that she had and was no better, but rather grew worse.

When she heard about Jesus, she came behind *Him* in the crowd and touched His garment. 28. For she said, "If only I may touch His clothes, I shall be made well."

Immediately the fountain of her blood was dried up, and she felt in *her* body that she was healed of the affliction.

And Jesus, immediately knowing in Himself that power had gone out of Him, turned around in the crowd and said, "Who touched My clothes?"

But His disciples said to Him, "You see the multitude thronging You, and You say, 'Who touched Me?'"

And He looked around to see her who had done this thing.

But the woman, fearing and trembling, knowing what had happened to her, came and fell down before Him and told Him the whole truth.

And He said to her, "Daughter, your faith has made you well. Go in peace, and be healed of your affliction."

Here we have a story of a woman who, according to verses 25 and 26, had been abused by the same circumstance in her life for twelve years. She not only lived with the affliction of the disease, but she also lived with the repercussion. We often live with not only our circumstances, but then we find that they also bring a lot of baggage, and things seem to just snowball. That is what she was going through. She suffered from her afflictions, and yet people abused her because of her affliction. She took her energy, her finances, and her time and placed them into the hands of physicians, only to have them abuse her and take advantage of her over and over again. The devil loves to take our trials and cause it to handicap us into believing that there is no other hope. She had become so desperate to be cured that she was willing to give it all to whomever to see results. I see so many people today that get messed up in the traps and seductions of the world because they are so desperate to be accepted and to be a part of something that matters in their life. Sadly, there is a generation that is turning to the deception of the world rather than to God because the devil offers a quick fix and a seductive lifestyle.

She became desperate for Jesus and the miracle that she needed in her life. The Bible doesn't tell us how many times she got knocked down, stepped on, and pushed to the back of the room. We all have been hurt and wounded by people who are not supposed to hurt us, but we must get desperate for God enough that we don't count how many times we got knocked down but instead we pursue God with desperation. It was her desperation that made the difference that day. When she touched the helm of His garment, power came from Him. God is not moved by needs—the world is full of people who have needs in their life—but he is moved by faith and people who are willing to get desperate. The disciples didn't even understand her desperation. There are people in our lives who will not understand why we are becoming so desperate for God, but they are the ones who are living without the power of God inside of them.

Sammy was a young boy who lived in the Deep South. His summer days were filled with times of walking through the woods, playing with friends, and fishing in the pond down the road. Fishing was by far his favorite thing to do. Just about every day during his summer vacation, he would dig up some worms and head off, pole in hand, for a day of fishing. This steamy, hot day was like most others during Sammy's summer break. Waking early, he could hear the pond calling him, "Come fish." Sammy quietly walked out the front door, grabbed his pitchfork and worm pail, and walked into the woods to search for bait. He turned over old stumps and dug under leaves, hoping to find worms. Under one old stump, he hit the jackpot. The ground was writhing. In two minutes, he had all the bait he needed; and in fifteen minutes, he was at the pond. Reaching into his bait bucket, Sammy pulled out a big worm. He double-hooked it and tossed in into the water. He noticed a stinging in his hand, but filled with the excitement of the moment, he paid no attention to it. Within thirty seconds, Sammy had a strike and pulled in a nice catfish. Wow, he thought, a fish in the first minute. He put the catch on his stringer, hurried to rebait his hook, and tried his luck again. Once again, he felt a stinging sensation in his hand as he threw his hook into the pond. He didn't have time to worry about it. Within just a few seconds, he had another huge fish. He fumbled the next time he baited his hook—his hand felt numb and stiff. But Sammy was too excited about catching another fish to give it much thought. At the end of only an hour, Sammy had caught eight large fish. This was definitely his best fishing day ever. He was so proud of his accomplishment that even though there was plenty of the day left to fish, he threw the heavy stringer of fish over his shoulder and dashed down the road toward home to show off his catch to his parents.

The local sheriff happened to drive up alongside Sammy and started to congratulate him on his catch of fish. With a smile and a victory whoop, Sammy held up the stringer. The sheriff gasped, parked his car, and ran over to Sammy. His eyes hadn't deceived him—Sammy's arms really were red and swollen to about twice their normal size. "Exactly where have you been, and what bait did you use to catch all those fish?" the sheriff asked Sammy.

"I found some special bait under an old stump," Sammy boasted. "The worms really wiggle good," he said, handing up the bucket for inspection. After a close look at the worms, the sheriff went into fast-forward. Putting the bucket in the car, he swooped up Sammy, made a U-turn on the dirt road, and sped off to the hospital; but Sammy was already dead. What the sheriff had discovered was that Sammy had been fishing with baby rattlesnakes. Sammy's deadly bait brought him a good morning of fishing but cost him his life. Had

Sammy stopped fishing after that first sting, he could have been saved. But Sammy was having to much fun and didn't bother himself with the small voice of pain in his hand. Then as the hand grew numb, even that voice was silenced. The devil loves to deceive us by giving us what we think we want. It's like using baby rattlesnakes for bait. It may seem harmless, but it's putting its venom in you, and it will affect you because sin will take you farther than you want to go. Sin will keep you longer than you want to stay! Sin will cost you more than you want to pay!

We get so desperate that we don't realize that we are killing ourselves and the purpose that God has for us. We often kill our destiny because we get desperate for what the world has to offer rather than for God. The woman with the issue of blood had gotten bitten everywhere she turned, and the Bible says she heard about *Jesus*! She became desperate to be awakened to a God that could not only heal her but forgive her as well. She pressed her way into the crowd, sick, weak, and abused; she began to crawl to Jesus. Desperate for something different, desperate to be accepted, and desperate to be loved, she fought at whatever cost to see an awakening in her life.

It's time that we get desperate for God. Think about that day that she finally touched Jesus. The place was full of people waiting to touch Him. Men, women, and children crammed into one place for one purpose. Have you ever been to Wal-Mart the morning of a big sale of a specific item? *Wow!* Talk about desperate people. It had to have been like that, or worse, that day that Jesus was in town. People were fighting, pushing, and shoving trying to see Him. In the midst of all of this chaos, a feeble, sick, and weak lady finds her way to the nucleus of the crowd and touches Jesus. Why? She was desperate for an awakening of God. The only account the Bible doesn't give us is how many times she was stepped on, pushed down, or shoved to the back of the room. I'm sure that day there were more people stronger than her or even bigger, but none more desperate. We often give up when we don't see immediate results. Just because someone or something comes in our way to keep us from our destiny we fall off the race because we can't get desperate enough for God. No one stood in proxy for her that day; she had to do it herself. The Bible says that when she touched Him, immediately her issue of blood dried up, and she was made whole, and there was an empowerment that came directly from Jesus that restored her body. It was such an enormous amount of power that it caught His attention. Jesus had been touching people all day, healing the sick, and ministering, as He always did, but someone got desperate. Desperation gets God's attention! When we become desperate to be awakened to our purpose and destiny, then there is restoration. It was her faith and determination that brought her to her miracle.

If we allow our circumstances to rule in our lives, then they will eventually kill us. If she had not changed her situation, she would have died. In 1880, James Garfield was elected president of the United States, but after only six months in office, he was shot in the back with a revolver. He never lost consciousness. At the hospital, the doctor probed the wound with his little finger to seek the bullet. He couldn't find it, so he tried a silver-tipped probe. Still he couldn't locate the bullet. They took Garfield back to Washington DC. Despite the summer heat, they tried to keep him comfortable. He was growing very weak. Teams of doctors tried to locate the bullet, probing the wound over and over. In desperation, they asked Alexander Graham Bell, who was working on a little device called the telephone, to see if he could locate the metal inside the president's body. He came, he sought, and he too failed. The president hung on through July, through August, but in September, he finally died—not from the wound but from infection. The repeated probing, which the physicians thought would help the man, eventually killed him. So it is with people who dwell too long on their wound and refuse to release it to God. They allow the infection of bitterness and unforgiveness to seep into the wound of their souls, and it eventually causes spiritual death. It's time we get desperate for God in our lives and quit hanging on to the things that are killing us!

BREAKING THE CURSE

CHAPTER 5

▼

BREAKING THE CURSE

Have you ever noticed that when you go to a doctor for the first time they always want to know if there have been any problems of sickness in your family? The same for insurance companies, they always ask, "Is there any diabetes, cancer, heart disease, hypertension, suicide, depression, etc.?" I have spoken to doctors and asked why families have generational sickness. Their answer is always, "We don't really know! We just know that there seems to be some hereditary factors that connect families down the generations." I see so many young people come into the Kingdom and God saves them, but there is so much baggage of the world from past generations that the devil discourages any growth; and soon they eventually wither away. If we are not careful, we will lose the generational blessings and replace them with curses.

A little girl called out, "Mommy, you know that vase in the china cabinet, the one that's been handed down from generation to generation?"

"Yes, dear, I know which one you mean, what about it?"

"Well, Mommy, I'm sorry, but this generation just dropped it!"

Now, some earthly possessions have sentimental value, and to break them is a great loss; but how much more tragic would it be for a new generation to "drop it" spiritually, to fail to pass along the godly heritage they have received! That would be an eternal loss. In Deuteronomy 6:1–3, Moses gave the Israelites instructions before they entered the Promised Land. The purpose was, in Moses's words, "You may fear the Lord Your God, to keep all His statutes and His commandments which I commanded you, you and your sons and grandsons, all the days of your Life." God's laws were to be observed from generation to generation. Moses, therefore, told the people, "You shall teach them diligently to your children and shall talk of them when you sit in your house, where you walk by the way, when you lie down, and when you rise up." He also instructed them, "You shall write them on the doorpost of your house and on your gates."

God wants to awaken us, but the truth is we often are distracted by the generational hand-me-downs from others in our family. We must conquer these generational territories by overcoming the curses and accepting the blessings in our lives. We don't know how to effectively deal with generational curses so that we can have an awakening with God.

Exodus 20:5

You shall not bow down to them or worship them; for I the LORD your God am a jealous God, punishing children for the iniquity of parents, to the third and the fourth generation of those who reject me, but showing steadfast love to the thousandth generation of those who love me and keep my commandments.

If you want to leave a lasting legacy for your children's children for a thousand generations, then give your life to Jesus and walk in His ways. However, the sin of your great-grandfather, grandfather, father (and mother) will have an effect on your life. That's why doctors and insurance companies always ask the above questions. What those people did affects you. What you do affects you and your children. The sin of your forefathers brings a curse.

Proverbs 26:2

As the bird by wandering, as the swallow by flying, so the curse causeless shall not come.

There is always a cause for the curse. God has laws, and they cannot be broken without consequence. Adam and Eve were the first to learn this:

Genesis 3:14–20

And the LORD God said unto the serpent, Because thou hast done this, thou art cursed above all cattle, and above every beast of the field; upon thy belly shalt thou go, and dust shalt thou eat all the days of thy life:

And I will put enmity between thee and the woman, and between thy seed and her seed; it shall bruise thy head, and thou shalt bruise his heel.

Unto the woman he said, I will greatly multiply thy sorrow and thy conception; in sorrow thou shalt bring forth children; and thy desire shall be to thy husband, and he shall rule over thee.

And unto Adam he said, Because thou hast hearkened unto the voice of thy wife, and hast eaten of the tree, of which I commanded thee, saying, Thou shall not eat of it: cursed is the ground for thy sake; in sorrow shall thou eat of it all the days of thy life;

Thorns also and thistles shall it bring forth to thee; and thou shall eat the herb of the field;

In the sweat of thy face shall thou eat bread, till thou return unto the ground; for out of it wasn't thou taken: for dust thou art, and unto dust shall thou return.

And Adam called his wife's name Eve; because she was the mother of all living.

When God created Adam and Eve, he blessed them, but the result of their sin brought a curse.

Verse 21 gives a hint to the breaking of the curse. "Unto Adam also and to his wife did the LORD God make coats of skins, and clothed them." So their covering or garment became what *identified* them. It was a symbol of their mistake and the sin in their lives. When God saw the garment, He saw redemption through the shedding of blood, but they saw that they were clothed because of their sin and mistakes. This was the first blood shed for sin in the Bible.

Mark 10:46–52

Now they came to Jericho. As He went out of Jericho with His disciples and a great multitude; blind Bartimaeus, the son of Timaeus, sat by the road begging.

And when he heard that it was Jesus of Nazareth, he began to cry out and say, "Jesus, Son of David, have mercy on me!"

Then many warned him to be quiet; but he cried out all the more, "Son of David, have mercy on me!"

So Jesus stood still and commanded him to be called. Then they called the blind man, saying to him, "Be of good cheer. Rise, He is calling you."

And throwing aside his garment, he rose and came to Jesus.

So Jesus answered and said to him, "What do you want Me to do for you?" The blind man said to Him, "Rabboni, that I may receive my sight."

Then Jesus said to him, "Go your way; your faith has made you well." And immediately he received his sight and followed Jesus on the road.

This is an amazing story, not just only about a miracle healing, but about generational curses being lifted and broken. In those days, people believed you were crippled or handicapped because of a sin of your parents or grandparents. People who had physical conditions were looked upon with disgrace and never given a chance to succeed in life. Here we have Bartimaeus, the son of Timaeus, who sat and begged by the road. Notice his physical placement was a direct result of his spiritual and emotional state as well. We all get that way! When we feel as if God is not moving in our lives in the spirit, we allow it to affect us in the physical. He sat in the physical, but he was also sitting in the spirit. We often sit spiritually and wait for God to zap us into His plan for our lives, but we fail to see that it is required of us to get up and change our environment. Bartimaeus was a fixture in the community; people expected him to be there begging and to be a bother.

Jesus shows up on the scene, and as He is ministering, Bartimaeus hears the Master speaking and begins to cry out to Him for mercy. The crowd immediately tried to silence him and keep him in his place. Society will never help you escape your generational curse. The media is designed to promote the negative and bring out what is not going right in our world. He begins to cry louder to get Jesus's attention and for Him to have mercy on him. After Jesus's attention is caught by the cry, He asks for Bartimaeus to be brought to Him. As Bartimaeus stands to make his way to Jesus, he does something very significant. He removes his garment.

I said earlier that the garment that Adam and Eve wore was a marking to them to indicate that they had sinned. It identified them as having broken the law of God. Bartimaeus wore a garment that identified him to the world. A cloak that would let people know that he was blind, so that they would not run him down in the street or that they would stop and give alms to him so he could make a living. This cloak was very important to his way of life. It was how he ate and survived. We all have come to depend on the curses in our lives as our crutch and our support. We don't give things to God because it's our little curse that we like to hold on to for our private pity parties. Bartimaeus knew that if he got that close to Jesus, then he wouldn't need this cloak anymore.

We should begin to understand that we have to remove what identifies us with the world and lay down curses that generations past have brought on us. Breaking mind control and eliminating thoughts that the flesh would try to get us to conform to is the only way to remove the garment in our lives. The Bible says in Romans 12:2, "And be not conformed to this world: but be ye transformed by the renewing of your mind, that ye may prove what is that good, and acceptable, and perfect, will of God." The only way to accomplish the breaking of curses is to be diligent in God's Word. Paul said spiritual metamorphosis is accomplished "by the renewing of your mind." The word *renewing* also means renovation.

Think of a house. You can make repairs. You know, the cosmetic kind—some paint and carpet—and it looks better, perhaps increases the resale value. But Paul isn't talking about repairing our minds. That may cover up some ugly defects for a while, but it isn't going to lead to transformation. You can restore a house to its original historic condition. You take out carpet and refinish the original wood floors. You find windows, doors, woodwork, and hardware in good condition from the period the house was built and install those to reverse someone else's "modernizations." But Paul isn't talking about restoring our minds to their original condition. We were born sinners and did not have the mind of God, so what is there to restore? Paul is talking about a complete renovation. This is not about cosmetic repairs or restoration. It's like taking a house and completely gutting it. Walls, floors, wiring, plumbing, cabinets, bath and kitchen fixtures, and roof—it's all completely new. Anyone who'd seen the house in its previous condition wouldn't recognize it now. That's what needs to take place in us according to Romans 12:2. Paul said something similar to the Ephesians: "Throw off your old evil nature and your former way of life, which is rotten through and through … Instead, there must be a spiritual renewal [renovation] of your thoughts and attitudes. You must display a new nature because you are a new person, created in God's likeness—righteous, holy, and true" (Eph. 4:22–24, NLT).

Rise Up You Bones

Ezekial 37

Chapter 6

▼

Rise Up, You Bones

The world is looking for God. Tragically and ironically, as the world is looking for God, God's people are asleep in their pews, asleep in religious traditions and lethargy. There is such a mandate and urgency in these last days for the church to rise up and take its place in the role that God designed only for us as believers, to take true possession of their territory

2 Chronicles 7:14

"If my people, who are called by my name, will humble themselves and pray and seek my face and turn from their wicked ways, then I will hear from heaven and will forgive their sin and will heal their land."

Ezekiel 37:1–10

Let's look at the history: God had called His people, the Jews, out of captivity in Egypt. For over one hundred years, they had been in Egyptian captivity. God brought them into the Promised Land and gave them a land and a king and made them a nation. *But* they turned against God, and God allowed them to go into captivity once again.

Nebuchadnezzar and his Babylonian army invaded Israel. They had reduced Solomon's Temple to ashes and had taken many of the Jewish people back to Babylon as captives. This is the condition that Ezekiel is in. The nation of Israel is *dead*. *But* God has a vision for Ezekiel.

37:1–2 Ezekiel is carried to a valley full of very dry bones. I want you to imagine this scene with me. These bones are scattered everywhere … very white … very dry. Bones all over the place … scattered by the wild animals so that there is nothing but miscellaneous bones as far as the eye can see.

For Ezekiel, this is a vision of the nation of Israel.

Ezekiel 37:11 There was no way that Israel could get themselves out of Babylonian captivity. They were like these dead, dry bones … in a graveyard, dead, in a hopeless situation.

Maybe this describes some of you or someone you know. You look around you, and it seems hopeless. Everything seems to have gone wrong. Your life is a mess, or at least it's not what you want it to be. You see yourself in a valley of dead, dry bones.

37:3a Look at the question. Ezekiel is looking at millions of dead, dry bones scattered about hundreds of square miles, and God asks him, "Can these bones live?" How would you answer that question?

When you look at your situation and all you see is a valley of dead, dry bones, you don't see much hope, do you? It's hard to imagine those dead, dry bones having life. It's hard to imagine your situation ever getting better. It's hard to imagine life beyond our present circumstances.

Israel has been taken captive by Babylon. Ezekiel can't see much hope for his people. However, he answers God's question in Ezekiel 37:3.

"Can these bones live?"

"I don't see how … if they do, it will be up to You, Lord!"

Ezekiel is telling God that God is in charge and in control. God can do whatever He wants to do. With God, nothing is impossible. If God wants these dead, dry bones to live, they'll live. Let's get relevant here. I see two areas where I see dead, dry bones—in our society, which is heading for destruction, and in the church, which thinks it is not headed for destruction.

What kind of bones do we see in the church today?

The Tailbone Christian—who just sits and lets everybody else do the ministry in the church. If God had wanted you to sit around and do nothing, He would have taken you on to glory the minute He saved you. 1 Corinthians 15:58 says, "Therefore, my beloved brethren, be ye steadfast, unmovable, always abounding in the work of the Lord, forasmuch as ye know that your labor is not in vain in the Lord."

"Can these bones live?"

Yes, as soon as they get off their tailbones! God wants to awaken us to get busy for the Kingdom and quit being idle to His will for our lives.

The Finger Bone Christian—who are always pointing their finger at everybody else, not taking responsibility for their own actions. They blame everybody else for the circumstances they find themselves in.

"Can these bones live?"

Yes, as soon as they see that they are reaping what they have sown. Psalm 7:16 says, "His mischief shall return upon his own head, and his violent dealing shall come down upon his own pate."

The Jawbone Christian—who runs off at the mouth, putting his mouth into motion before his brain is in gear. Who spreads gossip, which intentionally causes trouble by stirring up strife.

"Can these bones live?"

Yes, when they snatch their tongue from the devil and give it to the Holy Spirit. Ephesians 4:29 says, "Let no corrupt communication proceed out of your mouth, but that which is good to the use of edifying, that it may minister grace unto the hearers." Too long the body has done more damage to itself than the devil could ever do. We tend to self-destruct because we speak against each other rather than love one another and cause life to come back into the body. God wants to awaken us to our destiny and realize that everyone is in the body for a purpose and not just by accident.

The Hipbone Christian—who sits on his wallet every Sunday when the offering plate is passed in front of him.

"Can these bones live?"

Yes, when the heart is converted, the wallet will be converted too. Matthew 6:21 says, "For where your treasure is, there will your heart be also." Awakening of our dedication not just to be fed but to help feed. We often tithe to the government more than we do the Kingdom.

The Dry Bone Christian—whose Christian life has withered up because he/she isn't in the Word of God. We must not let ourselves become dry; we have to let the Word of God refresh us. There was a man who got lost in the desert. After he had been wandering around for a long time, his throat became very dry. About that time, he saw a little shack in the distance. He made his way over to the shack and found a water pump with a small jug of water and a note. The note read, "Pour all the water into the top of the pump to prime it. If you do this, you will get all the water you need." Now the man had a choice to make. If he trusted the note and poured the water in and it worked, he would have all the water he needed. If it didn't work, he would still be thirsty, and he might die. Or he could choose to drink the water in the jug and get immediate satisfaction, but it might not be enough, and he still might die. After thinking about it, the man decided to risk it. He poured the entire jug into the pump and began to work the handle. At first, nothing happened, and he got a little scared; but he kept going, and soon water started coming out. So much water came out he drank all he wanted, took a shower, and filled all the containers he could find. Because he was willing to give up momentary satisfaction, he got all the water he needed. Now the note also said, "After you have finished, please refill the jug for the next traveler." The man refilled the jug and added to the note, "Please prime the pump. Believe me, it works!"

We have the same choice to make: do we hold on to what we have because we don't believe there are better things in store for us and settle for immediate satisfaction? Or do we trust God and give up all that we have to get what God has promised us? I think the choice is obvious. We need to pour in all the water, trust God with everything. Then once we have experienced what God has to offer, the living water, we need to tell other people. "Go ahead prime the pump. Believe me, it works!"

"Can these bones live?"

Yes, when we immerse ourselves into the God's Word, the Water of Life.

The Wishbone Christian.-Remember when you were a kid and you got to pull on the wishbone of the Thanksgiving turkey? If you got the bigger piece, your wish was granted (supposedly). For some of us, that describes our prayer life—gimme, gimme, gimme. We come to God with our "wish list," and that pretty much describes our prayer life.

"Can these bones live?"

Yes, when we realize that prayer is a relationship with God that involves, not only asking, but thanksgiving, praise, fellowship, and worship.

The Backbone Christian—who has convictions, knows what they are, and stands on them. The Christian with *backbone* won't live his life to please the world or won't live her life to blend in with the world and won't live their life to conform to the standards of the world.

"Can these bones live?"

The individual activity of one man with backbone will do more than a thousand men with a mere wishbone. When the territories of life begin to place demands on our flesh, we must stand up in the face of peers and have the backbone we need to see the destiny of God in our lives. Yes, and they do live, as a testimony of the grace of God.

The Knee Bone Christian—who realizes that victory in the Christian life comes only through a life of praying.

"Much prayer, much power; little prayer, little power; no prayer, no power."

"Can these bones live?"

I believe that prayer is a vital key to the resurrection of our lives in Christ. What prayer is, prayer is coming into the presence of God. Prayer is entering the throne room of the King of Kings and Lord of Lords. Prayer is taking our concerns to the One who cares for us. Prayer is to stand on holy ground. Prayer is communicating with the Creator of the world (the One who spoke this world into existence with a word … mountains, oceans, stars). Prayer is a child talking to his Father. Prayer is bringing our hurts to the Father of compassion and the God of all comfort. Prayer is reaching out to our Redeemer. Prayer is crying out to the Rock that is higher than we are. Prayer is calling out to the only One who can save us. Prayer is touching the One who loves us with an unfailing and unquenchable love. Prayer is bringing our questions to the One who has the answers. Prayer is communication to a *never*, tired, confused, afraid, or taken by surprise God. Prayer is connecting our lives with the *All*-Knowing, *All*-Present, and *All*-Powerful King of Kings. Prayer is coming near to God. Moses told the people in Deuteronomy 4:7, "What other nation is so great as to have their gods near them the way our Lord is near us whenever we pray to him." Yes, and the knee bone Christian is the one who is living the life of *victory*.

I believe that there are three things that God wants to do to these bones in order to see a great awakening. In verse 6, it says, "And I will lay sinews upon you, and will bring up flesh upon you, and cover you with skin, and put breath in you, and ye shall live; and ye shall know that I am the LORD." Sinews are tendons. Tendons allow movement of the body. I believe in this great awakening of the Body of Christ. Then we must first begin to move out of the comfort zone that our flesh will sometimes place us in. In these last days, we must move outside of our own territorial boundaries and allow God to awaken us to our destiny. We must be willing to move and allow God to place spiritual tendons on our dry bones in order to move not only our lives but our environment. The second thing that I believe that God wants us to see before we can rise to the occasion is that He wants to give us flesh on our bones. This tells us that we have an identity in Him. Skin on bones gives us features that people recognize. The church at large has been overlooked in our society because of its lack of identity in God. We have been asleep too long, and it is time for the Body of Christ to rise up and take their identity. I see this so much in ministry—young people who are lost in the pool of a faceless generation and tend to just blend in. Public schools are becoming filled with faceless young people. God desires to awaken us to be who He has called us to be and not just blending in with everyone else. Then finally there is the breath. It was the breath that brings life. The truth is we are a dying people who desperately need to have the breath of God placed inside of them. God chose to breathe into Adam and complete His masterpiece. Breath is a sign of completion. When a mother is pregnant and the baby is born, it is the end of her pregnancy and the beginning of new, independent life. The doctor must cause the baby to cry to ensure that the child has breath, showing the completion of the birth. It is when God breathes into us that we have the completion of what we used to be and the beginning of a new awakening and destiny.

Ten percent of church members cannot be found? Twenty percent of church members never attend church, 25 percent admit that they never pray, 35 percent admit that they do not read their bibles, 40 percent admit that they never contribute to the church tithe or offering, 60 percent never give to missions, 70 percent never assume responsibility within the church, 85 percent never invite anyone to church, 95 percent have never won anyone to Christ. *But!* One hundred percent expect to go to heaven.

"Can these bones live?"

Yes, if we are willing to turn over every territory of our lives to God and allow Him to awaken our lives.

REMAINING

CHAPTER 7

▼

REMAINING

For a pastor, nothing is more frustrating than to see people on a constant roller-coaster ride in their spiritual walk. It is simply that God is too good for that. Don't misunderstand me when I say that there will always be ups and down in our lives because of the promise that Jesus Himself said in John 16:33. "In the world you will have tribulation; but be of good cheer, I have overcome the world." So the solution is not the removal of the ups and downs of our lives and the constant pressures of the world, but the ability to remain while experiencing these trials.

James 1:2–3

2 My brethren, count it all joy when you fall into various trials,

3 knowing that the testing of your faith produces patience.

It's our job to know that every test, no matter how big or small, will only produce the results that we allow it to. We must be awakened to the fact that the anointing of God is enough and can remain in our lives as real as the first day we felt Him. Calvin Coolidge said this: "Nothing in this world can take the place of persistence. Talent will not; nothing is more common than unsuccessful men with talent. Genius will not; unrewarded genius is almost a proverb. Education will not; the world is full of educated derelicts. Persistence and determination alone are omnipotent. The slogan 'Press on' has solved and always will solve the problems of the human race." It's about our willingness to remain in the anointing that God has for us.

John 15:16 says, "You did not choose Me, but I chose you and appointed you that you should go and bear fruit, and *that* your fruit should remain, that whatever you ask the Father in My name He may give you." It is a very important part of our destiny that we realize that our mandate from God is not what we would have chosen. The reality of it is that it is too big. If God were to reveal His complete plan for our lives to us, we all would probably run away from it all. So we did not choose the path for ourselves. God did, and all He asks of us to do is to simply remain on that path and allow Him to develop us. The concept sounds simple, but so many Christian get touched by God yet don't remain. God wants us to remain because we are the only ones that can bear fruit to the world of who Jesus can be to them. However, we find ourselves bearing fruit in our lives, but it's the wrong fruit.

1 John 2:27 says, "But the anointing which ye have received of him remains in you." According to this verse, the anointing never goes away and has no expiration date on it. If we truly receive the anointing, then it has no choice but to stay exactly where God placed it in our lives.

One of the greatest stories in God's Word concerning the anointing that remains is the awesome experience that Elisha had in his ministry.

2 Kings 2:1–14

1 And it came to pass, when the Lord was about to take up Elijah into heaven by a whirlwind, that Elijah went with Elisha from Gilgal.

2 Then Elijah said to Elisha, "Stay here, please, for the Lord has sent me on to Bethel." But Elisha said, "*As* the Lord lives, and *as* your soul lives, I will not leave you!" So they went down to Bethel.

3 Now the sons of the prophets who *were* at Bethel came out to Elisha, and said to him, "Do you know that the Lord will take away your master from over you today?"

And he said, "Yes, I know, keep silent!"

4 Then Elijah said to him, "Elisha, stay here, please, for the Lord has sent me on to Jericho." But he said, "*As* the Lord lives, and *as* your soul lives, I will not leave you!" So they came to Jericho.

5 Now the sons of the prophets who *were* at Jericho came to Elisha and said to him, "Do you know that the Lord will take away your master from over you today?"

So he answered, "Yes, I know; keep silent!"

6 Then Elijah said to him, "Stay here, please, for the Lord has sent me on to the Jordan." But he said, "*As* the Lord lives, and *as* your soul lives, I will not leave you!" So the two of them went on.

7 And fifty men of the sons of the prophets went and stood facing *them* at a distance, while the two of them stood by the Jordan.

8 Now Elijah took his mantle, rolled *it* up, and struck the water; and it was divided this way and that, so that the two of them crossed over on dry ground.

9 And so it was, when they had crossed over, that Elijah said to Elisha, "Ask! What may I do for you, before I am taken away from you?"

Elisha said, "Please let a double portion of your spirit be upon me."

10 So he said, "You have asked a hard thing. *Nevertheless,* if you see me *when I am* taken from you, it shall be so for you; but if not, it shall not be *so.*"

11 Then it happened, as they continued on and talked, that suddenly a chariot of fire *appeared* with horses of fire, and separated the two of them; and Elijah went up by a whirlwind into heaven.

12 And Elisha saw *it,* and he cried out, "My father, my father, the chariot of Israel and its horsemen!" So he saw him no more. And he took hold of his own clothes and tore them into two pieces.

13 He also took up the mantle of Elijah that had fallen from him, and went back and stood by the bank of the Jordan.

14 Then he took the mantle of Elijah that had fallen from him, and struck the water, and said, "Where *is* the Lord God of Elijah?" And when he also had struck the water, it was divided this way and that; and Elisha crossed over.

I think there are some awesome keys to finding, receiving, and remaining in the anointing in this passage of scripture. Let's first look at verse 4: Elisha had a passion to pursue the anointing. There was nothing that would stop him from the mandate that God had spoken to him that he would be the next chosen vessel to the people of God. What an awesome responsibility he must have felt. We get so caught up in the trap of the enemy that we find ourselves forgetting that we have a God-given anointing that is more than enough. Just as in verse 5, Elisha was not easily influenced by the talk of the people that surrounded him. We let people, circumstances, and our flesh talk us out of what God has given to us. Then a second time in verse 6, his faithfulness is tested. Please understand that the awakening of something big doesn't come without adversity and friction.

Then in verse 9, we see the anointing beginning to do what we all want it to do in our lives. It begins to meet his needs. How many times do we question "Why, God, is this happening or not happening to me?" Notice how the endurance of Elisha began to turn and pursue him. At this point, Elisha could have asked for anything he wanted and gotten it in an instant. He could have received a new house, a donkey, wealth. It didn't matter; the anointing was going to meet whatever he was in need of. Here is where he begins to allow the anointing to remain in his life. He chooses the one that he has been driving for and the lifeline, the thing that has caused him to stand in the face of adversity and talk of others; he simply chooses more of the anointing. We often find ourselves getting discouraged and burned out and going on to find something else to get us through when God said in John 15 to simply remain. So Elijah puts a stipulation to his request. He basically says to him in verse 10, If you want what you don't have, then move yourself to a place that you have never been. What an awesome thing to know that God wants to take us to a higher place with Him, not just to get us to move, but to place an even greater anointing on us. Elisha had to watch the anointing in order to be in the right place at the right time.

In verse 11, God comes for Elijah. Then Elisha sees the chariot and knows that this is his destiny, and he does a strange thing—he rips his clothes as the mantle of Elijah falls. We must get to the point that we are ready to remove the things that have us clothed now in order to take on what God has next. It was very symbolic that he tore the clothing because it was a sign that he would never wear those again. We cannot just lay down our rags of righteousness, but we must rip them so as to never wear them again. Verse 13 states that the mantle fell on him so he had to be exactly where the anointing fell. If you are not getting what others around you are getting, move to a place where you can receive it. Position is everything when the glory of God falls.

Psalm 133:2 talks about the anointing that flowed from Aaron's head down to his beard. It was custom in those days that the beard was symbolic of the maturity that one had. The beard being the closest thing to the head, this tells us that only the mature in Christ will stick as close to the head, where the anointing is being poured out. We must find someone that is operating in the anointing and place ourselves in the flow of the spirit, and that means letting down our pride and humbling our lives to the presence of God!

If we are not leaving something of God in each person we are called to serve, then we have missed the mark. God doesn't give us such a powerful anointing just for us to keep to ourselves. Long after we are gone, the anointing should still remain. It's that powerful.

2 Kings 13:20–21

Then Elisha died and they buried him. And the *raiding* bands from Moab invaded the land in the spring of the year.

So it was, as they were burying a man, that suddenly they spied a band *of raiders;* and they put the man in the tomb of Elisha; and when the man was let down and touched the bones of Elisha, he revived and stood on his feet.

This was an anointing so strong that even his bones still possessed the resurrection power of God. What an amazing truth for us: the presence of God that we have in our lives can remain if we allow it to. Everything Elisha accomplished in his life was due to the anointing, and it remained even after his death. This means that everything you come in contact with in your life has the potential to live because of the anointing that remains in you. The things that you maybe experiencing as a dry place or a dead time in your walk with the Lord can and will live if you allow the anointing and the fruit of your labor to line up with God's Word. My challenge to you is this: what are you doing with what God has given you! Elisha picked up the mantle in verse 14 and struck the water. He didn't waste any time—he put the anointing to use, and it remained.

Authentic Awakening

Chapter 8

▼

Authentic Awakening

Authenticity is one of the most coveted qualities in our society today. Everyone wants to have the original and have someone that is authentic and real. There is power in authenticity! I believe that the power of God in these last days will come through the people of God becoming more and more authentic in their relationship with Him. The days of lip service to God are done and gone. Satan himself is not scared of what we speak just with our mouths, but the reinforcement of an authentic relationship with God backs up and makes our words credible. The church as a whole has gotten comfortable with confessing Christ but cannot back up the authenticity of our relationship.

There are two guys in the Midwest United States that run a business of making doctor's note for people who need an authentic-looking excuse to get them out of work. People are paying top dollar for something that is supposed to represent an authentic reason as to why the employee is not coming to work. The world's search for authenticity is getting more and more desperate for the "real thing." The concept of authenticity covers every aspect of our lives. For instance, there is an authentic God, authentic Satan, authentic heaven, and authentic hell. So with all the authentic things and elements that make up our existence, then why are so many people *fake*? That's right, *fake!* We have more people trying to be something they are not and spending more time and energy on the copy rather than the original.

I believe that the only way to get into the authentic realm that God has for us is to hold the ticket of authenticity. God wants to awaken His people and call them to an undisputable, authentic place where we can fully and effectively do what He has called us to do. The entire world and our society are looking for the original and the authentic. Everyone wants to be the first to be good at something.

There are three keys to being authentic. The first is that we must realize that authenticity has uniqueness. There is only one original, and there are things that are unique to the authentic product. We can't fully show Jesus because we oftentimes are not real enough in our lives to portray the awesomeness of who God is. It is like the comparison of the light and darkness. John 1:5 says, "And the light shines in darkness; and the darkness did not comprehend it." The light is unique and has totally different characteristics than the darkness. When we are really awakened to God and what he has for us, it becomes evident to the world that we are different and unique.

A water bearer in India had two large pots; each hung on each end of a pole that he carried across his neck. One of the pots had a crack in it, and while the other pot was perfect and always delivered a full portion of water at the end of the long walk from the stream to the master's house, the cracked pot arrived only half full. For a full two years, this went on daily, with the bearer delivering only one and a half pots full of water to his master's house. Of course, the perfect pot was proud of its accomplishments, perfect to the end for which it was made. But the poor cracked pot was ashamed of its own imperfection, and miserable that it was able to accomplish only half of what it had been made to do. After two years of what it perceived to be a bitter failure, it spoke to the water bearer one day by the stream. "I am ashamed of myself, and I want to apologize to you."

"Why?" asked the bearer. "What are you ashamed of?"

"I have been able, for these past two years, to deliver only half my load because this crack in my side causes water to leak out all the way back to your master's house. Because of my flaws, you have to do all of this work, and you don't get full value from your efforts," the pot said.

The water bearer felt sorry for the old cracked pot, and in his compassion, he said, "As we return to the master's house, I want you to notice the beautiful flowers along the path." Indeed, as they went up the hill, the old cracked pot took notice of the sun warming the beautiful wildflowers on the side of the path, and this cheered it some. But at the end of the trail, it still felt bad because it had leaked out half its load, and so again it apologized to the bearer for its failure.

The bearer said to the pot, "Did you notice that there were flowers only on your side of the path and not on the other pot's side? That's because I have always known about your flaw, and I took advantage of it. I planted flower seeds on your side of the path, and every day, while we walk back from the stream, you've watered them. For two years, I have been able to pick these beautiful flowers to decorate my master's table. Without you being just the way you are, he would not have this beauty to grace his house."

Each of us has our own uniqueness. But if we will allow it, the Lord will use the power of our uniqueness to make us authentic.

The second key is power. Authenticity possesses power. If Bill Gates came into Wal-Mart, people would know immediately who he was. He possesses power because he was the originator of Microsoft Inc. Every person in the United States knows who Bill Gates is and what he started, and because of this, they treat him differently than other people because he is the author of something authentic. We must realize that God wants to release power into our lives as soon as we become real with Him and quit living a fake life.

The third key to authenticity is value. The sad truth is we often can't be real because we do not value our relationship with God. If I had an original Mickey Mantle rookie card, then I would have value because it was authentic. An authentic awakening with God will always add value to your life and cause you to place yourself in His perfect plan. There is an entire society out there that is begging for us to be real so they can experience an authentic God. We are not willing to do what it takes to have a relationship of value.

Pearls were perceived in the first century in much the same way we view diamonds today. They were the most valuable gem in the world at that time. If you owned a pearl, you owned a fortune. And there was a good reason for it. Pearl hunting involved immense danger. The fine-quality pearls were obtained from the pearl oyster. Since that oyster thrives at an average depth of forty feet, a pearl isn't a treasure you just stumble across as you walk along a beach. Pearls aren't found like that. In biblical times, they were obtained at great cost in terms of human lives—many people died while pearl hunting. They didn't have the equipment that's available today. First-century pearl-hunting equipment consisted of a rope and a rock. A pearl diver would tie a large rock to his body and jump over the side of a little boat, allowing the weight of the rock to carry him down to the oyster beds. He risked danger from sharks, moray eels, and other creatures to scour the mud below for oysters. An average of only one oyster in a thousand contains a pearl. All the while, he had to hold his breath and hope he wouldn't drown. You can see why pearls were so precious. The Jewish Talmud said, "Pearls are beyond price." The Egyptians actually worshipped the pearl, and the Romans copied that practice. When women wanted to show their wealth, they put pearls in their hair. When a Roman emperor wanted to show how rich he was, he would dissolve pearls in vinegar and then drink them in his wine. The diver realized the value of his lifestyle in that his benefits were that of reaping such a valuable resource that was coveted by so many people. The world wants the authenticity of a true God that we sometimes fail to put a value on.

Authentic means a) worthy of acceptance, as conforming to or based on fact; b) conforming to an original so as to reproduce essential features. Genesis 1:27 says, "So God created man in his own image, in the image of God created he him; male and female created he them."

When we begin to operate in the realm of the authentic, then we see the authenticity of who God really is. When you become authentic with Him, you then become worthy of acceptance based on the fact that He loves you. This will make you look just like Him with every essential feature. If you wonder why you don't see God the way that people around you see Him, it's because you are not authentic.

It is time that we are truly awakened in our lives to the one and only God that is more than enough for every trial and problem we may face. I hope this has challenged you to fully pursue God in a greater way, to be awakened from the inside and know that He desires to have a deeper relationship with you.